COPYRIGHT © 2024 By Simon Delaney.

All rights reserved.

ABOUT THE AUTHOR

The author grew up on a small estate and has faced numerous challenges throughout life, including learning difficulties, anxiety, depression, and other mental health struggles. For many years, they believed they weren't capable of achieving anything significant. However, with the support of Authors Solution UK, they discovered their potential and realized their goals. Once the book is published, the author plans to donate a copy to the NCHA project, where they once lived, to inspire others and show that no matter the obstacles, it's possible to achieve your dreams.

DEDICATION

To my family – my mum, my four sisters, nieces, nephews, and to Sky – for being the unwavering support that has guided me through every step of this journey. Growing up on a small estate, I faced many challenges, including learning difficulties and mental health struggles, and I often doubted my own potential. However, your love and encouragement showed me that anything is possible, and for that, I am forever grateful.

SPECIAL THANKS

To Authors Solution UK – thank you for providing the resources and support that allowed me to turn my dreams into reality. This book is proof that, despite any struggles or self-doubt, one can still reach their goals. I am honored to donate a copy to the NCHA Project, where I once lived, as a reminder that no matter the challenges, success is within reach.

TABLE OF CONTENTS

Waves of Change 1

Morning in the Village 2

The Market Square 3

The Traders' Arrival 4

An Island's Bounty 5

The Harvest Season 6

The Harvest Festival 7

The Ritual of Gratitude 8

Feasting and Merriment 9

The Children's Games 10

A Night of Celebration 11

A Time of Reflection 12

Legends of the Gods 13

A Church Adorned with Stories 16

A Sacred Altar 18

A Legacy for Generations 19

The Cycle of Life 20

Waves of Change

The waves of Nestra's pristine beaches whisper secrets of the sea. The gentle ebb and flow of the water have long guided the lives of those who call this island home. With every tide, the village reawakens to the same melody it has followed for centuries. Yet, despite this regularity, life in Nestra is never monotonous.

Before the first light touches the horizon, children scurry across the soft sands. They have been taught from a young age to appreciate the treasures the sea brings ashore—delicate seashells, gleaming pearls, and sometimes fragments of coral, washed up by the merciful waves. The island's artisans, who will later craft these finds into intricate pieces of jewellery and ornaments, depend on these early morning collections.

Despite their excitement, the children work quickly and efficiently, knowing they must return home before the village stirs. The laughter and whispered conversations among them are eventually drowned out by the sea's roar as it claims back the shore, erasing their footprints from the sand.

Morning in the Village

As dawn breaks, Nestra awakens slowly. Birds call from the lush forest that surrounds the village, their songs blending with the distant sound of waves. The village itself is modest, but its people take pride in their homes, each one built from materials harvested and crafted on the island. The scent of fresh bread wafts from kitchen hearths as families gather for breakfast—simple meals made from ingredients grown or foraged within the island's borders. Eggs, fish, fruits from the forest, and tea brewed from fragrant herbs are shared as conversations begin to flow.

In the quieter corners of the village, the elders sit together, sharing stories of the past. Their tales are the fabric of Nestra's identity, binding generations together. Around them, life unfolds. Young men and women prepare for the day's work—some heading to the fields, others to the sea. Many will make their way to the market square, where traders from distant lands are expected to arrive later in the day.

The Market Square

Nestra's market square is the heart of the village, a bustling hub of activity where commerce, culture, and community collide. Each morning, the market comes to life as vendors set up their stalls, displaying goods that range from freshly baked bread to pottery, textiles, and jewellery. The island's artisans take great pride in their work, and the quality of the goods reflects their skill.

For the villagers, the market is not just a place of business but a space for social interaction. Friends greet one another, families gather to shop, and children play games in the open spaces between the stalls. Today, however, there is a heightened sense of anticipation in the air. The distant sails of merchant ships are already visible on the horizon, and everyone knows that these traders bring more than just goods—they bring stories, news, and glimpses of the outside world.

The Traders' Arrival

By mid-morning, the first of the traders' ships dock at Nestra's harbour. The ships, with their wide, wind-filled sails, glide gracefully towards the shore, and as the traders disembark, they are met with warm greetings. Many of these traders have been coming to Nestra for years. The faces of the villagers are familiar to them, and over time, bonds have formed that go beyond simple business.

The traders bring with them goods that are not native to the island—spices that infuse the air with warmth, silks that shimmer in the sunlight, and gemstones that catch the eye with their brilliance. The exchange of goods is brisk, and the market soon fills with the scents and sights of faraway lands. Villagers crowd the stalls, eager to barter and trade.

Children weave through the throng, marvelling at the strange and wonderful items on display. For many of them, the arrival of the traders is the highlight of the month, a moment of excitement in the otherwise steady rhythm of island life. They listen intently to the conversations between the traders and their parents, soaking in the stories of distant lands where the mountains stretch higher than the clouds and the seas are as dark as night.

An Island's Bounty

While the market thrives, the fishermen of Nestra continue their work. The island is rich in marine life, and the sea has always provided generously for its people. Each morning, before the sun has fully risen, the fishermen take to their boats, casting their nets into the deep blue waters. Fishing is not merely an occupation here—it is a craft passed down through generations, an integral part of the village's way of life.

The catch today is plentiful—silver-scaled fish, lobsters, and crabs, all glistening under the midday sun. The fishermen return to shore, their boats laden with the bounty of the sea. As they haul their catch onto the docks, they are met by their families, who help sort and prepare the fish for smoking or selling at the market. Every part of the catch is used; nothing is wasted. What isn't sold or traded is preserved for the coming months, smoked over fires made from fragrant wood that imparts a unique flavour to the fish.

The fishing industry in Nestra is vital not only for the village's sustenance but also as a key component of trade. Nestra's smoked fish are sought after by traders, who carry them back to their own markets where they fetch a high price. The fishermen, while proud of their contribution to the island's economy, remain humble, quietly going about their work, knowing that the sea's gifts can never be taken for granted.

The Harvest Season

As summer stretches into autumn, the fields surrounding Nestra are lush with crops. Wheat, barley, and fruits ripen under the warm sun, and the farmers work tirelessly to ensure a good harvest. The agricultural cycle on the island is closely tied to the rhythms of nature, and the villagers know that each season brings its own challenges and rewards.

Harvest time is a community affair. Men, women, and children work together, gathering the crops and storing them for the winter months. The air is filled with the scent of freshly cut grain and ripe fruit, and the sounds of laughter and conversation as the villagers work side by side. The gods are always in their thoughts, and offerings are made at the shrines to give thanks for the bounty they have received.

As the last of the crops are brought in from the fields, the village prepares for the Harvest Festival, one of the most important events of the year. This celebration marks the end of the harvest season and is a time for the entire village to come together in gratitude and joy.

The Harvest Festival

The Harvest Festival is the crowning moment of the year in Nestra, a celebration that reflects the culmination of months of hard work and a time when the villagers come together to rejoice in the abundance of the earth. It is a moment when the island pauses to recognise the cycle of life, the blessings of the gods, and the strength of the community.

Preparations for the festival begin days, even weeks, in advance. The village square, which on most days serves as a bustling marketplace, is gradually transformed into a vibrant and festive scene. Colourful banners are strung between the buildings, fluttering in the breeze, while garlands of flowers—picked from the island's lush meadows—are draped across the tables. The entire village works together to prepare, each person contributing to the creation of a festival that honours their shared labour and devotion to the gods.

The square is filled with long tables, each one laden with the fruits of the villagers' work. Freshly baked bread, still warm from the ovens, is stacked in woven baskets. Roasted meats, seasoned with herbs from the forest, send tantalising scents into the air. Platters of fruits and vegetables, arranged in vibrant displays, sit beside dishes of freshly caught and grilled fish. Jugs of wine, fermented from the island's vineyards, and ale brewed from the barley harvested just weeks before, are placed within easy reach, ensuring that no cup remains empty for long. The mingling scents of roasting meats, spiced drinks, and baked goods create a rich, intoxicating atmosphere that draws everyone to the square.

The Ritual of Gratitude

Before the revelry begins, there is a solemn moment of reflection. The village elders, dressed in ceremonial robes woven from flax and dyed in shades of deep gold and green, lead the villagers in a procession to the shrine at the centre of the square. There, they offer the first fruits of the harvest to the gods—baskets filled with wheat, grapes, and pomegranates, along with flowers and precious stones gathered from the island's rivers. This offering is a symbol of the villagers' gratitude for the bounty they have received and a prayer for continued protection and prosperity in the seasons to come.

The villagers gather in silence as the elders raise their hands in prayer, their voices chanting the ancient words that have been passed down through generations. The gods are ever-present in the hearts of the people of Nestra, and this moment of offering connects them to the divine, reminding them that their success is not theirs alone, but a gift from the gods who watch over them. As the final words of the prayer echo through the square, the air seems to still for a moment, as though the island itself is pausing to listen.

Feasting and Merriment

As the sun begins to sink below the horizon, casting a golden light over the village, the festival officially begins. Musicians take their places, their instruments ready to fill the evening air with lively melodies. The music begins with the soft, lilting notes of flutes, soon joined by the deep, rhythmic beats of drums and the twanging strings of lyres and lutes. The sound is infectious, and soon the square is filled with the joyous movement of villagers dancing in time to the music.

The dancers, dressed in brightly coloured clothes woven specially for the occasion, twirl and spin through the square, their feet tapping out the rhythm of the music. Some wear crowns of flowers, while others have draped themselves in ribbons of crimson and gold. The joy is palpable, their movements reflecting the freedom that comes with the end of the harvest, a time when the hard work of the year is behind them and the fruits of their labour can be fully enjoyed.

Villagers, dressed in their finest attire, join in the dancing, their laughter ringing through the square as they link arms and move together in time with the music. The energy is contagious, and even the elders, who normally watch from the sidelines, find themselves drawn into the festivities. Their faces glow in the firelight as they sway gently to the music, content in the knowledge that their village is thriving.

The Children's Games

For the children of Nestra, the Harvest Festival is a time of unbridled joy and adventure. Freed from their usual chores and responsibilities, they run wild through the square, their imaginations fuelled by the stories of old. They wield wooden swords and shields, engaging in mock battles as they pretend to be the heroes of the village's legends. In their minds, they are mighty warriors, slaying monsters and defending Nestra from unseen foes. Their laughter mixes with the music, creating a symphony of life and celebration that echoes throughout the village.

Some of the older children organise races and games, dashing between the tables and leaping over barrels. Their laughter is loud and carefree, a reminder to all who watch that the future of the village is bright, held in the hands of these spirited young souls. The younger ones, dressed in their festival best, chase after fireflies as dusk falls, their tiny hands reaching for the glowing lights that dance through the air. The village dogs, sensing the excitement, weave through the crowd, tails wagging as they chase after the children in playful abandon.

For a moment, as the children's laughter fills the air, the adults are reminded of their own childhoods, of festivals long past, when they too played under the stars with the same unbridled joy. There is a sense of continuity in these moments—a passing of the torch from one generation to the next.

A Night of Celebration

As the night deepens, the festivities continue. The music grows louder, and the dancing becomes more exuberant. Torches are lit, casting flickering shadows across the square, and the bonfires that were prepared earlier in the day are finally set alight. The flames leap high into the night sky, their warmth pushing back the cool autumn air. The villagers gather around, their faces illuminated by the glow of the fire, their hearts warmed by the shared sense of community.

Around the bonfire, stories are told—tales of the gods, of great battles, of ancient heroes who once walked the island. The village storyteller, an elder with a voice as rich as the sea itself, weaves these legends into vivid tapestries that capture the attention of both young and old. His words, paired with the crackling of the fire, create a magical atmosphere. As he speaks of the gods who protect the village and the ancestors who built it, the villagers are reminded of their place in the grand story of Nestra.

The feast continues long into the night. More food is brought out from the kitchens, and the wine and ale flow freely. As the villagers eat, drink, and celebrate, there is a palpable sense of gratitude in the air—gratitude for the land that has provided, for the gods who have blessed them, and for the community that has worked together to make it all possible.

A Time of Reflection

As the night wears on, the festival begins to quieten. The children, exhausted from their games, are carried home by their parents, their heads resting on their shoulders as they drift into peaceful sleep. The musicians play slower, more reflective melodies, and the villagers, full from the feast, sit by the fire, sharing quiet conversations with one another.

In these moments of calm, the villagers reflect on the year that has passed and the challenges they have overcome. There is a sense of pride in the air—pride in the work they have done, pride in the village they have built, and pride in the knowledge that they have faced adversity together and emerged stronger for it. The Harvest Festival is not just a celebration of abundance; it is a reminder of the resilience of the people of Nestra, of their ability to weather any storm and come out the other side with full hearts and open hands.

As the final embers of the bonfire die down and the last notes of music fade into the night, the villagers slowly begin to make their way home. The square, which had been alive with colour and sound just hours before, now lies still, the tables empty and the torches burning low. But the spirit of the festival lingers, carried in the hearts of all who were there. For in Nestra, the Harvest Festival is more than just a feast—it is a celebration of life itself, a reminder that through hard work, unity, and faith in the gods, the village will continue to thrive for generations to come.

Legends of the Gods

No festival in Nestra would be complete without the telling of the village's most cherished stories—the legends of the gods who protect them. As the evening grows darker and the bonfires are lit, the villagers gather around, eager to hear the tales once more.

The most famous of these legends tells of the four gods—Alus, Amiulas, Sepis, and Anika—who descended from the heavens to save Nestra from destruction. Long ago, a great evil rose from the depths of the earth, bringing with it an army of twisted creatures. The village was on the brink of ruin when the gods appeared, their golden armour gleaming in the sunlight, their swords flashing as they fought off the invaders.

Alus, the warrior god, led the charge, his strength unmatched by any foe. Amiulas, goddess of the harvest, ensured that the land remained fertile even in times of hardship. Sepis, god of the sea, calmed the waters, allowing the fishermen to continue their work. And Anika, goddess of prosperity and joy, brought peace to the village, ensuring that its people would never go hungry or without hope.

The village of Nestra stands as a place deeply rooted in tradition, its people devoted to the gods who have watched over them through countless generations. This devotion is manifest in the numerous shrines that dot the island, each one a testament to the gods' protection and guidance. These shrines, though simple in construction, are sacred spaces where villagers pause in their daily lives to offer prayers and gifts in thanks for the blessings they have received. The scent of fresh flowers and incense often drifts from these altars, mingling with the natural fragrance of the island, creating an atmosphere of serenity and reverence.

At the heart of the village, however, stands the grandest of these shrines, a larger, more elaborate structure that serves as the spiritual centre of the island. Here, the villagers gather for significant religious events, festivals, and collective prayers. The shrine is a place of reflection, where villagers come to seek solace in times of hardship and offer their gratitude in times of plenty. Its stone façade, worn smooth by the elements, reflects the enduring faith of the community.

Recently, in an extraordinary show of unity, the villagers undertook an ambitious project— one that would honour the gods and future generations alike. They set about building a new church, a grand structure that would not only serve as a place of worship but also as a symbol of their resilience and commitment to one another. This was no small undertaking, and the entire village was called upon to contribute. Farmers, fishermen, artisans, and labourers all lent their hands, working tirelessly to ensure that the new church would be a fitting tribute to their shared beliefs.

For months, the sounds of construction filled the village—hammers striking nails, stone being chiselled, and the rhythmic beat of workers as they moved in unison. The building process became a communal act of devotion, a way for every villager to feel personally connected to the project. Each brick was laid by hand, with care and precision, symbolising the strength and unity of the village itself. Even the children were involved, fetching water for the workers and bringing food to sustain them throughout the long hours of labour. In the evenings, as the sun set behind the horizon, the workers would pause to admire their progress, knowing that they were creating something that would stand for generations to come.

The construction of the church wasn't merely an architectural feat— it was a spiritual one. The very act of building became a form of worship, with each villager pouring their love and dedication into every stone, every beam. Old and young, men and women, all worked side by side, united in their shared purpose. The project, which took many months, was completed with immense pride and joy. As the final stone was laid and the roof raised, a sense of accomplishment washed over the village. The church now stood as a testament not just to the gods, but to the enduring spirit of Nestra's people—a symbol of their resilience, their unity, and their hope for the future.

A Church Adorned with Stories

The church, when finally completed, was a marvel to behold. Its stone walls, cool and solid, rose high into the sky, casting long shadows across the village square. But it was inside that the true beauty of the structure revealed itself. As one entered the sanctuary, the space opened up to a series of intricate murals that adorned the walls. These murals, painstakingly painted by the village's most skilled artisans, depicted the legends and myths of Nestra's gods.

Each image told a story. There was Alus, the warrior god, standing tall with his sword raised high, a protector of the island's soldiers and defenders. His figure was painted with bold strokes, his golden armour gleaming in the sunlight that filtered through the stained-glass windows. Next to him was Amiulas, goddess of the harvest, her arms outstretched, offering wheat and fruit to the people. She was painted in softer tones, her figure surrounded by images of farmers toiling in the fields, their crops thriving under her watchful gaze.

Sepis, god of the sea, was depicted in shades of blue and green, his form fluid and powerful as he calmed the waves that crashed against the shores of Nestra. In the mural, fishermen cast their nets into the ocean, their boats rocking gently on the waves. Sepis was their guardian, ensuring safe passage and plentiful catches. And finally, there was Anika, the goddess of prosperity and joy, surrounded by dancers, musicians, and villagers in the midst of celebration. Her mural was alive with movement, the vivid colours of the festival scenes capturing the spirit of the island's many joyous occasions.

The light that streamed through the stained-glass windows only enhanced the beauty of these murals. Each window was a masterpiece in itself, depicting scenes from the village's history—battles fought and won, bountiful harvests, and moments of divine intervention. The coloured glass cast vibrant hues of red, gold, and blue across the stone floor, creating an almost ethereal atmosphere within the church. The villagers who entered the space felt a sense of peace and connection, not only to their gods but to their ancestors, whose stories were now immortalised in art.

A Sacred Altar

At the centre of the church stood the altar, carved from the finest wood that the island's forests had to offer. The craftsmen had worked tirelessly to ensure that every detail was perfect, from the intricate carvings of vines and leaves that wound their way around the edges, to the smooth, polished surface that reflected the light of the candles that always burned there. The altar was the focal point of the church, a place of reverence where villagers came to offer their prayers, their hopes, and their thanks.

Here, offerings were laid each day. Flowers, freshly picked from the forest, their petals still wet with morning dew, were arranged in delicate patterns. Fruits, carefully harvested from the fields and orchards, were placed in bowls of carved stone. Gems, rare and precious, found in the rivers and streams of the island, were laid at the altar as a symbol of the villagers' gratitude for the wealth the land had provided. The villagers believed that through these offerings, the gods would continue to bless them with good fortune, protection, and prosperity.

The church had quickly become more than just a place of worship—it was the heart of the village. Here, life's most important moments were marked. Newborns were brought to the altar to receive the blessings of the gods, and marriages were celebrated with grand ceremonies, the air filled with the scent of flowers and the sound of music. The church was also a place of solace during times of hardship. When crops failed or storms battered the island's shores, the villagers gathered here, seeking comfort and guidance from the gods.

A Legacy for Generations

The completion of the church marked a new chapter in the history of Nestra. It was not only a physical structure but a lasting symbol of the village's shared values. Every brick, every beam, every mural within its walls held the story of a people bound together by faith, community, and a love for the land that sustained them. The church would stand for generations, its walls bearing witness to the lives of those who built it and those who would come after.

And so, with the church complete and the gods honoured, the villagers of Nestra looked to the future with hope. They knew that as long as they remained true to their traditions and worked together in harmony, their village would continue to thrive, protected and blessed by the gods they held so dear.

In Nestra, the past, present, and future were woven together in a tapestry of faith, community, and resilience—a legacy that would endure for many lifetimes to come.

The Cycle of Life

Life in Nestra flows in harmony with the turning of the seasons, each bringing its own challenges and gifts, as predictable as the tides but no less impactful. The island's rhythms are attuned to nature's clock, and the villagers have long learned to embrace the ebb and flow of their environment, trusting that every season holds its purpose.

Spring, the season of renewal, awakens the village from its winter slumber. The fields, which lay dormant under the mild chill of the colder months, are now abuzz with activity. Farmers, their tools polished and their spirits refreshed, venture out at first light, scattering seeds into the fertile soil. The air is sweet and fragrant, filled with the scent of blossoming flowers and the fresh greenery that carpets the forests. Songbirds return to their nests, filling the air with cheerful melodies, their presence a reminder that life is bursting forth anew.

The forests, too, are alive with growth. The trees, bare and skeletal during the winter, begin to flourish, their branches heavy with buds that will soon burst into a riot of colour. The villagers walk the forest paths, marvelling at the transformation. Foragers set out to gather wild herbs, berries, and mushrooms, the fresh abundance of the earth offering its bounty once more. Children chase after butterflies, their laughter carried on the breeze, as the island comes alive in a vibrant display of renewal.

Summer brings with it the season of toil, when the days stretch long and the sun hangs high in the sky. The work is hard but deeply satisfying. Villagers rise with the dawn, knowing that every moment counts as they tend to the growing crops. The sun, though often merciless, shines a golden hue over the fields, where wheat and barley stand tall, swaying gently in the breeze. In the gardens, vegetables flourish under the watchful eyes of their caretakers, while fruit trees, heavy with promise, begin to show the first signs of ripening.

The sea, warm and inviting, also offers its gifts in abundance. Fishermen set out early in the morning, their boats cutting through the clear waters as they cast their nets into the deep. The ocean's bounty is plentiful in the summer months, and the fishermen return with their boats laden with fish, crabs, and other treasures of the sea. The day's catch is brought to the smokehouses, where the fish are carefully prepared, salted, and preserved to be enjoyed throughout the rest of the year.

Though the summer days are long and the work demanding, the villagers find joy in the shared labour. They work side by side in the fields, their hands calloused from the soil and their bodies tanned by the sun. There is laughter amidst the toil, and in the evenings, when the work is done, they gather in the village square to share meals, stories, and companionship. The long summer nights are filled with the sounds of music and conversation, a reminder that even in the busiest season, there is time for connection and celebration.

As summer's heat begins to fade, autumn arrives with the rich colours of harvest. The fields, now heavy with crops, are a sight to behold—a testament to the hard work and dedication of the villagers. The golden hues of the wheat and barley contrast with the deep greens of the forests, where the leaves have begun their gradual shift to red and orange. Autumn is a season of plenty, and the village buzzes with activity as the crops are gathered and stored.

The harvest is a communal effort, with men, women, and children all lending a hand. The sounds of scythes cutting through grain, the clatter of carts filled to the brim with produce, and the joyful shouts of villagers echo through the air. There is a palpable sense of achievement and pride, knowing that the village has secured enough food to sustain them through the colder months ahead.

The autumn air is crisp, carrying with it the first hints of winter. Yet the coolness is refreshing, invigorating the villagers as they prepare for the coming celebrations. The Harvest Festival is a time of joy, a chance for the entire village to come together in gratitude for the year's bounty. The square is transformed into a scene of feasting and revelry, with tables laden with freshly baked bread, roasted meats, and sweet, spiced pies. Jugs of wine and ale are passed around freely, and the sound of music fills the night as the villagers dance and laugh under the stars.

Winter, while milder than in many other lands, is a time of quiet reflection in Nestra. The fields, once vibrant with life, now rest under a blanket of frost, the soil allowed to rejuvenate. The trees, stripped of their leaves, stand tall and bare against the grey sky, their branches swaying gently in the cold winter wind. Life slows down, and the villagers retreat indoors, gathering around warm fires to share stories of old and prepare for the coming spring.

Though the days are shorter, the slower pace of winter offers the villagers a rare opportunity to rest. The hard work of the previous seasons has ensured that there is enough food stored away to last through the winter, and the fireside becomes the heart of each home. Families come together to mend clothes, craft tools, and tell tales of the past, their bonds strengthened by the shared warmth of the hearth. The village's artisans, who worked alongside the farmers in the warmer months, now turn their attention to their crafts, producing beautiful pottery, textiles, and jewellery to trade when the warmer weather returns.

Winter, though peaceful, is not without its own form of celebration. The villagers mark the turning of the year with the Winter Solstice Festival, a time when they honour the gods and give thanks for the protection and abundance they have received. Small gifts are exchanged, and the village square is once again lit by bonfires, the flickering flames casting long shadows as the villagers gather to sing songs and offer prayers for the new year.

Through each season, the villagers of Nestra remain united. Their lives are inextricably linked to the land and the sea, and they have learned to trust in the cycles of nature, knowing that each season has its own place in the greater whole. They work hard, but they also find joy in their shared labours and in the knowledge that they are part of something much larger than themselves—a community that has endured for generations, bound together by history, tradition, and a deep reverence for the gods.

The gods, ever-present in the minds and hearts of the villagers, are honoured in every season. Spring brings offerings of flowers and fresh herbs, laid at the feet of the gods' shrines in thanks for the renewal of the earth. In summer, the first fruits of the harvest are brought to the altar, a symbol of gratitude for the abundance of the land. Autumn's celebrations are centred around the harvest, with the gods honoured for their protection and guidance throughout the growing season. And in winter, the villagers offer prayers for a safe and prosperous year ahead, knowing that the gods will watch over them through the darkest nights.

The village of Nestra is more than just a place—it is a way of life, a testament to the enduring strength of community and the power of tradition. Its people, deeply connected to the land, the sea, and each other, live in harmony with the natural world, trusting in the cycles of life to guide them through the challenges and rewards of each season. As the seasons turn, so too does the village continue to thrive, each generation building upon the legacy of those who came before, and ensuring that the spirit of Nestra endures for years to come.